Sweet Pea & Friends
Brave Little Finn

By John and Jennifer Churchman

L B

LITTLE, BROWN AND COMPANY
NEW YORK   BOSTON

One cold winter morning, a shy little lamb was born. "We'll call you Finn," said Farmer John. He held Finn close, keeping him warm inside his green barn jacket.

Finn had been born early and wasn't as strong or as big as the other lambs. He shivered against the icy wind as they made their way up the hill to the warm farmhouse.

Farmer John whispered in his soft, fuzzy ear, "Be brave, Little Finn. We're all here for you…always."

Finn's big sister Sweet Pea visited him every day, even when it was windy and cold. She would put on her favorite wool scarf and come up to the farmhouse to see how he was doing and tell him all the barn news.

Little Finn spent his days by the warm fireplace and made friends with the dogs and new puppy. While living inside, he had to wear a diaper! Finn thought he might look silly, but all the dogs agreed he looked quite nice.

Farmer John fed
Little Finn from a baby
bottle. Maisie Grace, the
border collie puppy, taught
him how to drink from it.

On sunny days, he enjoyed curling up on a bed of hay in the greenhouse. As winter turned to spring, Little Finn grew stronger.

One morning, he was finally ready to go outside and meet the other lambs. Finn was feeling nervous. What if no one liked him?

"Be brave, Little Finn," said Maisie Grace. "I'll be here with you."

Atticus, Meadow, and Hayzel were excited. They could not wait to meet Finn and hear all about being raised in the farmhouse! They planned to show him the drinking pond first, and then all around the pasture.

First the lambs stopped at the pond for a drink. Finn bent down for a sip of cool water but was startled by a pair of bright green eyes looking back at him. What was that?

Keeper the goose was floating nearby. "Little Finn," she honked, "don't worry. That's just Pond Frog staying cool in the shade. He sings his beautiful songs for us each evening."

Next, Little Finn's new friends took him to the lilac bush. Hayzel and Meadow loved the lilacs and munched and munched. But Finn was unsure. He had never eaten anything purple before. *What if they taste bad?* he worried.

"They're so sweet!" said Meadow, her mouth full of purple flowers and green leaves. "Please try some, Finn. They're a special spring treat," said Hayzel.

He took just a tiny nibble. They were delicious!

The next morning, Little Finn felt something
wet and cold on his wool coat. It was raining!
He was scared. What should he do?
Where should he go? He did not like being wet!

Puddle the duck was out early, splashing and flapping. "Come and play with me in the fresh rain," she quacked happily. Finn headed out to play with her. He was surprised—splashing in the rain really was fun!

When summer came, the whirring and buzzing sounds in the air worried Little Finn. He carefully stepped through the garden flowers. The butterflies were beautiful, but the hummingbird had such a long and pointy beak, and he had heard that bees could sting!

He saw his friend Atticus, who had stopped to nibble a rose. "No need to be worried about the things that fly and buzz, Little Finn," said Atticus. "They pollinate the plants, which helps Farmer John grow flowers, fruits, and vegetables."

Finn looked up and smiled.

"Come see the Big Round Bale of Hay," the lambs said excitedly. "In the fall, we'll play Lamb on the Mountain to see who can climb to the top!"

All the lambs loved watching Maisie Grace jump from one bale to the next.

Oh my, worried Little Finn. *I could never climb that high.* But fall was still weeks away. He hoped he would be brave enough by then.

One morning, Little Finn looked out the barn door and noticed something new—a hat! The hat had not been there the night before. He quickly turned around and went back inside the barn, and would not come out.

Sweet Pea loved hats of all kinds. Wearing her favorite bonnet, she gently urged Little Finn to come out. Finn cautiously tried on the straw hat. *This isn't so bad,* he thought. He felt quite grown up.

Early the next day, while taking a morning walk with Laddie the sheepdog, Little Finn noticed a large web. Then he saw a spider! "Spiders are so scary," Finn whispered to Laddie.

"There's no need to fear Miss Spider," said Laddie. "She's an artist, weaving her web. Look how pretty it is." Little Finn studied the intricate web sparkling with morning dew, and he was not so afraid anymore.

Finn peered into the darkness of the old barn and saw something else strange. Was that a MONSTER hiding in there? He ran as fast as he could and bumped right into Sadie the pony.

Sadie gave a soft neigh. "Oh, Little Finn. That's just Old Ford the tractor. He's resting in the barn after a long summer of farmwork. He pulls the wagon that holds all of our hay for winter."

Finn loved eating hay. Still, he stayed away from Old Ford.

One cool fall night, Little Finn could not sleep.
Soon it would be time to climb the Big Round
Bale of Hay. He didn't feel ready.

Even the sky looked scary. As the full moon rose high, Finn saw it get
covered by a dark shadow! His knees started to quiver. "Why is the moon
getting dark?" he whispered to Grandfather Snow, the wise old ram.

"That, my young Finn, is a lunar eclipse," said Grandfather Snow.
"You are a lucky lamb to be awake for this rare and wonderful sight."

"I don't feel lucky," said Finn.
"I'm afraid of everything."

"But what happens when you
get scared?"

"My friends are there to help me,"
said Finn. Grandfather Snow smiled
and drifted off to sleep.

Tomorrow was a big day. Finn was still nervous but knew he would have to try his best.

He thought about all his friends, especially Maisie Grace and Atticus, and how they would all be cheering him on.

Finn felt just a little bit...brave.

When morning arrived, everyone was very excited.
Maisie Grace, Laddie, Cyrie, and Quinn had come to watch.

Hayzel cried, "Everyone gets a turn!" All the lambs tried and
tried, but no one could make it to the top.

Little Finn tried, too. "You can do it, Finn!" called his friends. He
took a deep breath and ran and leaped and dug his hooves in.
He made it all the way to the top of the Big Round Bale of Hay!

"You are the brave and mighty Little Finn!" all his friends cheered.

That night, as he enjoyed his bedtime snack and lay down to sleep in the barn with his friends all around, Little Finn remembered the promise Farmer John had whispered in his ear. *"Be brave, Little Finn. We're all here for you…always."*

He felt very brave and loved, because he knew it was true. His friends would be there for him, and he would be there for them, too.

The True Story of Finn

Twin lambs Finn and Hayzel were born on a cold, twenty-below-zero winter night. Their mother, Blossom, did not have enough milk for them, so both were very weak. Hayzel bounced back quickly with bottle feeding, but Finn continued to get weaker and needed around-the-clock care in the farmhouse. When Finn was just a week old, our veterinarian, Alison Cornwall, sat at the table in the kitchen with him on her lap to deliver the results of his exam. "It's going to take a miracle to bring this little guy through," she said.

We were not going to give up on him! So we spent the next few weeks taking care of Finn in the farmhouse, bottle-feeding him warm milk and changing his diapers. Neighbors and friends came to help and to hold him. Despite our best efforts, he took a turn for the worse and lost the ability to drink from a bottle. John started "intensive-care feeding," and Jennifer worked with herbalists and the vet to find ways to keep him healthy until he got strong enough to eat solid food.

Our wonderful online community was following Finn's story and sent suggestions for herbal remedies, notes of loving encouragement, and wishes and prayers. The dogs would let Finn curl up on the dog bed with them for security and warmth. Our puppy, Maisie Grace, took a personal interest and would encourage Finn to move around, or just cuddled up with him whenever she could. Later, she was the one who taught him how to eat solid food from a bowl (she had just learned herself!).

Finn bravely fought on, slowly growing stronger. When he was finally able to eat grass on his own in the yard, we all breathed a sigh of relief: We had our miracle. Just as we've shown in the book, Finn was very shy and cautious when he joined the other lambs (he really was even afraid of John's hat!). We were so inspired by how the other animals helped him that we knew we had to tell his story.

Farmer John feeding Finn his bottle

Resting with Laddie

A warm jacket and a diaper

Little Finn with the dogs

Maisie Grace and Finn having breakfast

Behind the Scenes: The Art of *Brave Little Finn*

From a very young age I was always drawing, painting, and taking photographs. To my teachers' dismay, I would not "color inside the lines" and was quite happy to chart my own creative path. One of my earliest memories is taking pictures of our family dog with a Kodak Instamatic camera. In college I studied English, though photography, studio art, and theater also filled my time. The summer of my sophomore year marked a turning point in my life. A near-death experience brought me closer to what I feel is my true purpose—creating art and telling stories. The world looked different, more alive and vibrant, with a new depth and meaning. As my art evolved over the years, I found myself combining the mediums of painting and photography. Although each has always influenced the other, combining the two in photo illustration has brought my work, and my own artistic expression, to an exciting new level.

The art of *Brave Little Finn* was inspired by the beauty of nature, including all the conditions of light through the seasons: frost patterns and wisps of ice that form on the window, the play of sunlight through a mist of rain, leaves floating on water, dewdrops on spiderwebs, how moonlight changes the landscape. Living on our small country farm and surrounded by nature and the animals that bring joy to my life, I'm able to watch their interactions and individual personalities, and my visual stories begin to unfold. The illustrations in this book were created by arranging layer upon layer of my photographs, blending them digitally as I would layer paint on a canvas by hand. As I combine images, the story starts to appear just as I envisioned it. I am fortunate to be able to work with my wife, Jennifer, weaving words together with the images to create these stories of the life that surrounds us on Moonrise Farm. It is my greatest joy to be able to share this view of the world with you.

—John

Playing in the yard

Jennifer giving Finn a lift

A Special Thanks

This book was created with the support and encouragement of friends, family, and followers of Finn's story online. We would like to thank our agent, Brenda Bowen; editors, Megan Tingley and Allison Moore; and the whole team at Little, Brown Books for Young Readers.

The story doesn't end here! Join Sweet Pea & Friends for more adventures at sweetpeafriends.com.

Finn checking on Maisie Grace during nap time

Finn feeling better

Dedicated with love to our children,
Kailie, Travis, and Gabrielle

Little, Brown and Company

Hachette Book Group
1290 Avenue of the Americas, New York, NY 10104
Visit us at lb-kids.com

Little, Brown and Company is a division of Hachette Book Group, Inc.
The Little, Brown name and logo are trademarks of Hachette Book Group, Inc.

The publisher is not responsible for websites (or their content) that are not owned by the publisher.

First Edition: October 2016

ISBN 978-0-316-27359-6

10 9 8 7 6 5 4 3 2 1

1010

Printed in China